For The Fabulous 4 — Sammy, Ella,
Daisy, and Rosie! — xx's
— R.H.H.

To Buddy, for guarding the sketches —
by sitting on them!!
— N.H.

The illustrator wishes to acknowledge
Evan Sult, her production consultant.

Text copyright © 2005 by Bee Productions, Inc.
Illustrations copyright © 2005 by Nicole Hollander

Little, Brown and Company

Time Warner Book Group
1271 Avenue of the Americas, New York, NY 10020
Visit our Web site at www.lb-kids.com

First Edition: November 2005

Library of Congress Cataloging-in-Publication Data

Harris, Robie H.
  I'm all dressed! / Robie H. Harris ; illustrated by Nicole Hollander. — 1st ed.
      p. cm. — (Just being me)
  Summary: A little boy does not want to get dressed for his grandfather's birthday party, but if he must wear
clothes, he will put them on in his own unique way. Includes brief notes on handling a child who wants to have his
own way.
  ISBN 0-316-10948-7
  [1. Clothing and dress — Fiction. 2. Individuality — Fiction. 3. Behavior — Fiction. 4. Parent and child — Fiction.] I.
Hollander, Nicole, ill. II. Title. III. Series: Harris, Robie H. Just being me.
PZ7.H2436Iabc 2005 [E] — dc22

                                                                                                2004019961

10 9 8 7 6 5 4 3 2 1

IM

Printed in China

The illustrations for this book were done in pen and ink. Color was added using Adobe Photoshop.
The text was set in Providence and Sylvia (designed by Nicole Hollander and Tom Greensfelder),
and the display type is Drunk Cyrillic.

just being
me

I'm ALL

Dressed!

By Robie H. Harris

Illustrated by Nicole Hollander

LITTLE, BROWN AND COMPANY

New York ❧ Boston

"It's snowing out!" I shouted. "I love snow!"
"So does Grandpa!" said Daddy.

"You need to get dressed for Grandpa's birthday party," said Mommy.
"I don't want to," I said. "I like me like this!"

"You can't go to the party in underpants," said Daddy.
"Why not?" I said.
"Because it's snowing out," said Daddy.

I like my underpants.

I like them too, but...

"O-kaaaay...," I said. "I'll get dressed."
I wiggled and squiggled as Mommy
dressed me. She put on my sweatshirt,
my sweatpants, and my socks.

I PUT ON MY SNOW boots — ALL BY MYSELF!

I squirmed when Daddy zipped up my snow jacket,
pulled on my hood, and tied a scarf around my neck.
Then I put on my mittens—all by myself!
"Let's go!" I said.

I looked out the window.
The snow was blowing.
The wind was howling.

So I took off my mittens, untied my scarf,
yanked off my hood, and pulled off my jacket.

"It's late!" said Daddy. "We'd better help get you dressed again—fast."
"No!" I yelled. "Don't dress me!
I can dress me—

all by MYSELF!"

I grabbed my sweatshirt
and put my legs through the arms.

I grabbed my sweatpants
and put my arms though the legs.

I wound the scarf around my waist.
I tied the legs of my snow pants around my neck.

And I wrapped my jacket around my bottom.

I put a mitten on each foot and a sock on each hand. Finally, I pulled my snow boots on my feet and put a hat on my head — and ran to the living room. "Look at me!" I said.

I'm Dres

"Oh no!" said Daddy.
"You can't go dressed like that!"

"But he's ready to go," said Mommy.
"And we can't be late for Grandpa's party!"
"Well...he IS all dressed...," said Daddy. "So let's go."
"Wait!" I said. "I'm NOT all dressed!"

And I ran to my room, got my
sunglasses, and put them on.

Then I ran to the front hall mirror and looked at me—and smiled. I liked the way I looked!
"NOW—I'm ready to go to Grandpa's birthday party!"

Mommy opened the front door.
The snow was still blowing.
The wind was still howling.

"It's SO windy!" said Daddy.
"It's SO cold!" said Mommy.

"It's NOT cold!" I shouted. "And I'M not cold! I'm toasty warm. 'Cause I dressed me MY way!"

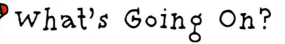

What's Going On?

When young children insist that they need little or no help from a grown-up to dress themselves, they are taking a big step toward becoming independent. And when they choose which clothes they want to wear, they are making a statement of how they see themselves and how they want others to see them. Getting dressed "their way" helps children see themselves as unique, with individual likes and dislikes that may be different from those of their parents, brothers or sisters, or friends.

Parents may often find themselves trying to balance their enjoyment of their child's individuality and newfound skills with the necessities of daily life, from accommodating the weather to keeping to a schedule. In this story, the boy's first choice to wear underpants has little to do with the cold and snow outside; it is about how he feels at that very moment. His parents' explanation that it is "very, very cold" outside encourages the boy to let his parents dress him in the appropriate clothes. Understanding that young children and adults often have a very different sense of time, the boy's parents are able to finish dressing him quickly by letting him put on the clothing he can easily manage — his boots and mittens.